# The Secret of the King

♛

*To my own special children of the King—*
*Jordan, Cassi, Cátia, Kaiden, Jared, and Liana.*
*And to my husband, TJ, who is a true knight.*
—RACHEL ANN NUNES

*To my two young knights-to-be—Chandler and Mark Alan—*
*and to my wife, Jileen, the princess of our home.*
—JAY BRYANT WARD

Special appreciation to Young Living Family Farm for the use of their costumes, props, and inspiring Medieval Village.

Many thanks to Jeffrey D. Ward for assistance on the artwork.

Text © 2005 Rachel Ann Nunes
Illustrations © 2005 Jay Bryant Ward

Some illustrations may reflect imagery from Corel Stock Photography.

Visit us at shadowmountain.com

Library of Congress Cataloging-in-Publication Data

Nunes, Rachel Ann, 1966-
    The secret of the king / Rachel Ann Nunes ; illustrated by Jay Bryant
Ward.— Two medieval children long to become knights in the king's army,
but they learn that they can be just as valuable doing other things.
        p.   cm.
ISBN 1-59038-241-2 (hardbound : alk. paper)
[1. Middle Ages—Fiction.  2. Knights and knighthood—Fiction.]  I. Ward,
Jay Bryant, ill.  II. Title.
PZ7.N9644Se 2005

[E]—dc21                                                                    2004025775

Printed in the United States of America                                          42316
Inland Press, Menomonee Falls, WI
10   9   8   7   6   5   4   3   2   1

# The Secret of the King

## of the

# The Secret KING

### · RACHEL ANN NUNES ·

ILLUSTRATED BY JAY BRYANT WARD

SHADOW
MOUNTAIN

Javan and Lia peered out of the bushes as the King's army passed the outskirts of their village. The knights were especially impressive, looking big and brave in their shiny silver armor. They rode tall, strong horses in two straight lines behind the King. On poles high above their heads waved the King's banners.

Javan imagined himself inside the armor, staring out at the world through the heavy metal visor. He would love to feel the weight of the sword at his side. Oh, how he would fearlessly battle any foe of the King!

"I wish I could go with them," he whispered.

"Me, too," Lia whispered back.

Both shared the same dream—to join the army of the King. Usually, the dream was far from reach. But today as they watched the knights and foot soldiers march into the forest, it seemed much closer than before.

"Javan!" The shout came from far away.

Javan groaned. Had Silvan noticed he was missing? Both Javan and Lia should have been at their chores hours ago, but they had come here instead to watch the army march by.

Lia glanced behind him, her blue eyes bright in the morning sun. "Silvan will be wanting you at the smithy," she said. "And I had best get to the bakery. If the army returns, we'll need more bread."

Javan gave a last glance at the knights and soldiers, now almost out of sight. With a long sigh, he stood and brushed the leaves from his clothing.

"They will win," Lia said fiercely.

"Of course," Javan answered. "I just wish we could be a part of it."

In silence they ran toward the town.

Javan hurried to the smithy, where he spent the morning pumping the bellows and pounding red-hot iron with a huge hammer. He had done so every day of his life since he came to apprentice at Silvan's shop five years ago. Silvan was a kind master who had taught him many things. But Javan didn't want to be a blacksmith. He wanted to be a knight in the King's army.

Silvan did not believe in Javan's dream. "The army needs horseshoes more than they need another soldier or knight. Come, let us make as many as we can."

For days after the army had passed, Javan heard nothing about the war. He did his work with a heavy heart. He wanted to fight beside the King, not hide in the hot smithy like a coward.

Each evening, Javan and Lia practiced with Silvan's swords in the village square. Lia was good at darting in and out. Javan, with his arms grown strong from working in the smithy, was good at direct, hard blows.

One evening as the sun sank into the forest, Javan and Lia were again practicing with the swords. Suddenly, Javan heard the rushed clip-clop of hooves on the cobblestones in the village square. A helmetless knight cried out for help as he nearly toppled from his horse.

Javan and Lia dropped their swords and came running. "Quick, grab him!" Javan cried. They caught the knight as he fell.

"The doctor!" shouted Javan. "Lia, get the doctor! I'll stay with him."

Lia ran for the inn, her blonde braid flying behind her.

Javan struggled under the knight's weight. The man moaned as Javan laid him on the ground. "What happened?" Javan asked urgently.

"Fighting . . . battle," said the knight, his eyes shut tight with pain.

Javan gasped. "We are losing?"

The knight opened his eyes. "Lose—never! But we need . . . help. The King sent me . . . I was . . . wounded on the way." His eyes closed.

Javan saw a jagged hole in the knight's armor. By the look of his pale face, the knight had lost a lot of blood.

As Lia spread the word, villagers poured from the inn and houses. They gathered around the knight, who struggled to his feet. He could stand only by leaning heavily upon Javan and the doctor.

"I have come in the King's name," he said. "We must have supplies for our army."

"We are ready," said Silvan. "We will send the supplies you need."

The knight nodded his thanks, but Javan became angry. "What he really needs are more soldiers!" he shouted. "We should put on the King's armor and fight with swords!" The villagers around Javan and Lia gasped and began to murmur among themselves.

"What do we know of fighting?" asked the baker. "We have no training."

"We must stay with our families," said the innkeeper.

Lia met Javan's eyes. "They're afraid," she whispered. "They're all afraid."

Javan thought so too.

"Tell us," Javan asked the knight, "doesn't the King need soldiers?"

"The King is accepting soldiers," the knight replied. "A new group is gathering at the camp even now to go to his aid. All those who wish may join."

Silvan shook his head. "We'll help in the way we know how. The King needs supplies for his army—that is important. While the others pack the wagons to make the journey around the forest, I'll go to the King to tell him help is coming. I will set out this instant."

Javan saw his chance. "I'll go!" he said. "Let me deliver the message!"

Silvan frowned at them. "You are more useful here. The soldiers need metal to repair their armor and more horseshoes for their horses. And without bread they will not have strength for victory."

"You and the others can take care of that," Javan said. "Lia and I want to really *do* something. We want to fight in the King's army."

Silvan bowed his head. "Very well. But remember, Javan, there are many ways to wear the King's armor and to fight in this war." The other villagers nodded their agreement.

"They are just saying that," Javan told Lia quietly. "You were right. They are afraid."

Javan and Lia each quickly packed a small bag. Silvan gave them horses to ride. He also gave them his swords. They set off rapidly into the darkening night, following the directions the knight had given them.

"Will we arrive in time?" asked Lia, peering into the trees.

"I am certain of it." Javan felt very brave and important. He had visions of reaching the battle and of fighting so faithfully that the King would make him a knight. He would

wear shiny armor, live in a castle, and spend his free time fighting evil dragons. Maybe he would even save a princess or two. Finally, he would be doing something other than wasting time making tools and horseshoes.

"And I won't have to bake bread," Lia said when he told her his thoughts. "We'll be the most famous, bravest knights the King ever had."

They were deep in the forest when they heard a baby crying. Javan was tempted to ride by, but Lia directed her horse toward the sound. In a small clearing off the main path they found a group of young children outside a small shack. One girl held a crying baby in her arms, her own face slick with tears.

A boy stood up from where he'd been sitting on a fallen log. "Please, we are so hungry," he said. "Do you have food? Our father and older brother are fighting with the army, and our big sister went hunting for roots and berries yesterday and hasn't returned."

Lia nodded. "I have flour in my bag. Javan, go inside and build a fire in their hearth so I can bake them some bread." Lia worked quickly, kneading the flour with the water they'd brought in their flasks. She made a large loaf of flat bread for the children to eat now and several more loaves for later. Then she kissed the littlest child before mounting her horse.

"We must leave," Javan told them. "We are going to fight in the King's army."

"No doubt our sister will soon return to tend us," the boy replied. "May you find

At last they were riding in the forest again. Night had long since fallen while they had cared for the children, but the bright moon overhead shone through the trees onto their path.

"Do you think we're too late?" Lia asked. "Perhaps the new volunteers for the King's army have left without us."

Javan shook his head. "No, there is still time. We will make it."

As they neared the far edge of the forest, they heard another cry. "Help! Oh, help! Please, will anyone help me?"

Neither Javan nor Lia wanted to waste more time, but the plea sounded too desperate to ignore. Javan pointed to a thicket. "The cry came from there."

Lia nodded. "I'll light the lantern so we can see."

Behind the thicket they found a dark-haired maiden lying on the ground, her face streaked with tears. Next to her stood a large dog bearing several fresh wounds.

The maiden stared up at Javan and Lia. "Help me, I beg you! My foot is caught in this animal trap, and I cannot escape! My dog is also wounded from fighting off wolves. I fear he cannot withstand another attack."

Javan had seen similar traps in the smithy and knew how they worked. Quickly, he dropped to his knees and freed the girl. Then Lia bandaged her ankle with a handkerchief.

Javan and Lia turned to leave, but the maiden hesitantly touched Lia's sleeve. "Please, did you see a shack in the forest? I need to find my brothers and sisters, but I am quite turned around and do not know the way."

Just keep walking on this path," Lia told her with a touch of impatience.

The girl nodded, staring at their swords. "You must be going somewhere very important."

Javan lifted his head proudly. "We go to serve in the King's army."

"The King!" The girl gave a little bow. "I hope you are made knights, for I know you will fight bravely." She took a few halting steps down the path, grimacing with pain. Her dog limped slowly after her.

Javan met Lia's eyes, and with a sigh she nodded.

"Maiden," Javan said to the girl, "we will take you back to your brothers and sisters."

The girl sighed with relief. "Oh, thank you! I am most grateful."

By the time Javan and Lia left the girl with the children, dawn was filtering through the trees. "I think we are too late," Javan said sadly.

"Maybe not," Lia answered.

But Javan was right. When they arrived at the King's camp, the new volunteers were gone. Only wounded soldiers and a doctor remained.

Lia wiped tears from her cheeks and wouldn't look at Javan. He felt miserable. They had come all this way for nothing.

"We shouldn't have stopped," Javan said.

Lia sighed. "How could we not? The girl, the children—they needed us."

"Yes, but now we have failed the King."

Suddenly a group of knights came galloping into the camp. Their armor was dented, and some of their horses limped badly.

"Call the blacksmith!" cried a knight with a red feather in his helmet. "We need new shoes for our horses, and our armor needs repair. We are also weary with hunger."

"The cook and the blacksmith are gone," replied the doctor. "They rode off to join the army. But I can take care of your wounds."

The knight thanked him as he leaned heavily on his sword. "Did they not know how much we needed them here? I had hoped they might have received supplies," he said. "Has no village come to our aid?"

Javan stepped forward. "Our village is sending help. The wagons must go around the forest, but they will be here soon. We were sent to tell the King."

"Then we will return to the battle until they arrive," said the knight with the red feather. "I trust we will find the strength."

Javan wanted to go with them, but he realized that another soldier was not what they needed. He took a deep breath. "Sir," he said, "I know how to help your horses. I can replace their old shoes. If there is some metal in your blacksmith's wagon, I can repair your armor and even make new horseshoes."

"I know how to make bread," Lia offered. "Your cook must have a few supplies left. And I can help sharpen your swords while the bread bakes."

The knight bowed to them. "We gratefully accept your offer."

Javan and Lia worked more quickly than they had ever worked before. They did not want to disappoint the knight with the red feather. He walked tirelessly among the other knights, giving them encouragement. Never once did they see him rest or even remove his helmet.

Before long the horses were ready, the food hot, the swords sharpened, and the armor repaired. The grateful knights left them and returned to the battle. More knights and soldiers came to the camp for food and repairs to their armor. Javan and Lia forgot their sadness at not being in the army as they worked to help and comfort those who needed them.

Just when their meager supplies ran out, the wagons from their village arrived. Javan gave a prayer of silent thanks for the tools, horseshoes, and flat pieces of metal Silvan had sent. Lia was grateful for the flour, which she used to make the bread that gave the knights and soldiers strength. The villagers had also sent cheese, fruit, new stones for sharpening swords, and a promise of more supplies.

Sometimes Javan and Lia gazed at the armor of the knights with longing but only for a moment. There was much work to be done.

At last the day came when the trumpets sounded in jubilation, and the army returned. The victory banner waved high for everyone to see. Javan and Lia were happy the army had seen victory, but they also felt sad, wishing they had helped win the battle.

To their great surprise, the King approached, his purple robes flowing behind him. Javan and Lia fell to their knees.

The King leaned over and laid a gentle hand on each of their heads. "Please arise."

Javan at once recognized the voice as that of the knight with the red feather. He could barely look at the King in his shame. "I'm sorry we didn't make it on time," he said, blinking back tears.

"Yes," Lia added in a small voice. "We really wanted to fight in your army."

A smile appeared on the King's face. "Oh, but you did." He pointed to Javan's singed vest and Lia's flour-dusted apron. "You are even now wearing my armor, and I am very proud of you." He slipped his arms around their shoulders. "But even closer to my heart," the King said, his eyes gleaming with emotion, "you saved the lives of my own precious children, whom I had hidden in the forest from the enemy."

Following his gaze, Javan and Lia looked up to see the dark-haired maiden and the children riding into the camp, accompanied by several knights. As they reached the King, the smallest boy jumped eagerly into his father's awaiting arms. Warm happiness entered Javan's heart. Lia laughed with joy.

I believe," the King added, "that you have both learned the secret of what it means to be true knights in my army. Come. Let us go to the celebration together."